Enid Blyton

The Wizard's Magic Needle

Illustrated by RENE CLOKE

DERRYDALE BOOKS
NEW YORK

THE WIZARD'S MAGIC NEEDLE

THERE was once a wizard called So So, who had a wonderful needle. He had only to speak to it and it would start sewing anything he wanted.

If he said "Needle, make me a bag," it would make one.

If he said "Needle, make me a coat," it would at once set to work to make him one out of any old rag.

Now one day Curly Toes the pixie
wanted some sacks for his potatoes. He
couldn't afford to buy any, so he thought
he would make some out of some old
pieces of carpet that he had. But when
he had finished making one sack, he was
very tired indeed, for he hated sewing.

"If only I could borrow So So's
needle!" he thought, "how fine that
would be! I should only say Needle,
make me a sack and it would make me
one at once. All I should have to do would
be to sit and watch it!"

He made up his mind
to go to wizard So So's
and ask him for the loan of
his magic needle. So he
put on his hat and set out.
He knocked at So So's
door, and the wizard
opened it.

"Will you lend me your magic needle?"
asked Curly Toes.

"Certainly not," said So So. "I never
lend it to anyone. It is far too valuable"

He slammed the door and left Curly Toes
on the step, frowning hard.

The pixie was
setting off home
again when he
happened to catch
sight of the needle on
a table just inside So So's kitchen window.
"Ho!" he thought, "there's the
needle itself! What's to prevent me from
taking it and using it without the wizard
knowing? I can easily put it back again
when I have finished with it, and he won't
be any the wiser!"

With that the naughty
pixie slipped his hand
through the open
window, picked up the
needle and ran off!
It wasn't long before
he was home again.

He took all the pieces of old carpet and laid them in a row on the floor. Then he put the magic needle in the middle of them.

"Needle, make me some sacks!" he said.

At once the little needle got busy. It jumped to a piece of carpet, and in a second it had sewn one piece into a fine sack.

There was a
long thread always
sticking out of the
needle and it used
this to sew the sack
together. It was
really wonderful
to watch.

Curly Toes enjoyed
it all thoroughly.

It was fine to sit
down at the table
and see the needle
doing all his hard
work. He would
have plenty of
strong sacks for
his potatoes.

In five minutes the needle had used up
all the pieces of carpet, and had made six
good sacks.

Curly Toes waited
for it to put itself
quietly down beside
them, then he meant
to pick it up again
and take it back to
So So's house.

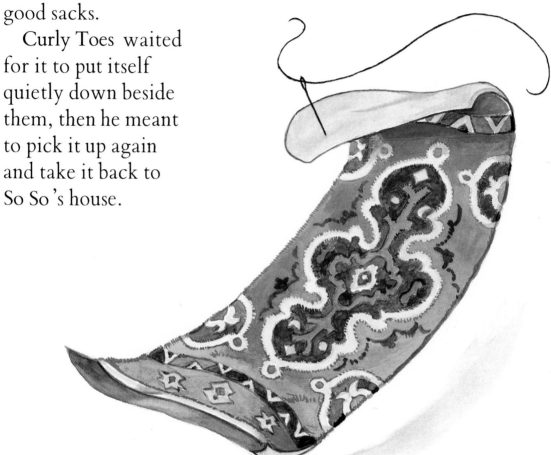

But the needle didn't stop sewing! To
Curly Toes great surprise, it whipped up
the lovely new rug on the floor and began
to make a sack of that too!

"Hey!" said Curly Toes,
angrily. "Stop, needle!
That's my new rug!
Don't spoil it! I don't
want any more sacks now."

The needle took no notice at all. It
just went on sewing the rug into a sack.
Curly Toes rushed up to it and tried to
stop it. It pricked him hard on the finger
and he howled with pain.

"Oh, you horrible needle!" he wept. Why don't you stop when you're told to? Stop, I tell you, stop!"

The needle still took no notice. It finished making a sack of the rug and then pulled down one of Curly Toes pretty red curtains and began to make that into a sack too.

The pixie couldn't bear it. He had made
the curtains himself and he wasn't going
to have them all spoiled.

He took a pair of
pliers and went softly up to the needle.

He suddenly pounced on it and caught it in the pliers. But it wasn't and good at all!

The needle slipped out quite easily and gave the pixie such a jab in the arm that he danced round the room in pain.

The needle took down the other curtain and made a sack of that too. Then it hopped on to the table and Curly Toes gave a cry of rage.

It was going to make his lovely blue table-cloth into a sack as well!

"You can't, you mustn't!" he cried. "I received it for my birthday and you won't spoil it!"

He climbed on to the table and sat
himself firmly down in the middle of the
cloth to stop the needle from making it
into a sack. But it wasn't a bit of
good!

In a second, the cloth was being sewn into a sack -and, oh dear me, what was happening?

Curly Toes suddenly found him-self sewn tightly into the sack too! The needle pulled the neck of the sack tight and sewed it carefully all the way round. Then it flew out of the window!

Poor Curly Toes! He sat in the middle of the table, sewn tightly into a sack made of his blue table-cloth.

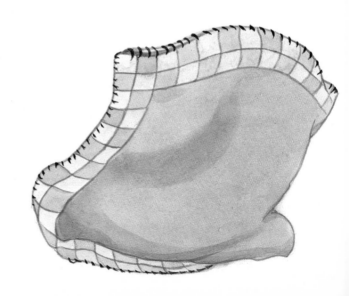

He struggled and
wriggled, shouted and cried. But he
couldn't get out of that sack!
Soon his friends heard his cries and
they came running to his aid.

How they laughed to see the pixie
in such a fix!
They got some scissors and tried to cut
the stitches open round the neck of the
sack. But they couldn't! The thread
was magic, and try as they would, they
couldn't cut or break it.

"Well, Curly Toes, this is a fine thing!"
said his friends. "We can't set you free!
You will have to go to Wizard So So's and
ask him to help you. Come along, we will
go with you."

So poor Curly Toes was helped off the
table and then he hopped slowly out of
his front door, for
it was impossible to
walk in the sack.

He could
do nothing
but jump.

He kept tumbling
over and, really, it
was the funniest
sight, though the
pixie didn't think so.

At last he arrived at the wizard's house,
and So So opened the door. How he
laughed to see the pixie in a table-cloth sack!

"Yes, I know what
you've done!" he said.
"I saw you take my
needle, but I knew it
would punish you, so I didn't say
anything. How are you going to get out
of that sack?"
"Do please help me!" begged the pixie.
"Certainly not," said the wizard.
"You got yourself into this fix, so you
must get out of it yourself too."

"Oh, do help him, So-so," begged all Curly Toes' friends. "He is very, very sorry."

"Well, if I get you out of the sack, will you come and weed my garden every day for a week?" the wizard asked Curly Toes.

Now the pixie hated weeding, but he couldn't do anything else but agree. So he said he would. Then So So fetched a pair of magic scissors and – snip-snip! The stitches were all cut, and Curly Toes was free!

Off he went home and spent the rest of
the day trying to undo the stitches in his
rug and curtains.

He went to bed
a very sad pixie.

Then every day for a week he set off to
weed the wizard's garden and, by the
end of that time, he had learnt his lesson.

"I'll never, never borrow anything without asking!" he vowed. And, as far as
I know, he never did!